Crash! Bang! Boo!

ALSO IN THE JUNIOR MONSTER SCOUTS SERIES

JUNIOR MONSTER SCOUTS

#2 Crash! Bang! Boo!

By Joe McGee
Illustrated by Ethan Long

ALADDIN

NEW YORK   LONDON   TORONTO   SYDNEY   NEW DELHI

This book is a work of fiction. Any references to historical events, real people, or real places are used fictitiously. Other names, characters, places, and events are products of the author's imagination, and any resemblance to actual events or places or persons, living or dead, is entirely coincidental.

ALADDIN

An imprint of Simon & Schuster Children's Publishing Division
1230 Avenue of the Americas, New York, New York 10020
First Aladdin paperback edition September 2019
Text copyright © 2019 by Joseph McGee
Illustrations copyright © 2019 by Ethan Long
Also available in an Aladdin hardcover edition.

For information about special discounts for bulk purchases, please contact Simon & Schuster Special Sales at 1-866-506-1949 or business@simonandschuster.com.
The Simon & Schuster Speakers Bureau can bring authors to your live event.
For more information or to book an event contact the Simon & Schuster Speakers Bureau at 1-866-248-3049 or visit our website at www.simonspeakers.com.
Cover designed by Karin Paprocki
Interior designed by Mike Rosamilia
The illustrations for this book were rendered digitally.
The text of this book was set in Centaur MT.
Manufactured in the United States of America 0719 OFF
2 4 6 8 10 9 7 5 3 1
Library of Congress Control Number 2019931558
ISBN 978-1-5344-3680-0 (hc)
ISBN 978-1-5344-3679-4 (pbk)
ISBN 978-1-5344-3681-7 (eBook)

FOR JESSICA,
ALWAYS
And for our own
Junior Monster Scouts:
Zach, Ainsley, Shane, Logan,
Braeden, and Sawyer

★ ★ ★ ★

Finally, for the late, great
Stan Lee (1922–2018)

*The more you read, the better you're
going to become as a storyteller.*
—Stan Lee

Thank you, Stan, for filling the world
with heroic stories.

· THE SCOUTS ·

VAMPYRA may be a vampire, but that doesn't mean she wants your blood. Gross! In fact, she doesn't even like ketchup! She loves gymnastics, especially cartwheels, and one of her favorite things is hanging upside down . . . even when she's *not* a bat. She loves garlic in her food and sleeps in past noon, preferring the nighttime over the day. She lives in Castle Dracula with her mom, dad (Dracula), and aunts, who are always after her to brush her fangs and clean her cape.

WOLFY and his family live high in the mountains above Castle Dracula, where they can get the best view of the moon. He likes to hike and play in the creek and gaze at the stars. He especially likes to fetch sticks with his dad, Wolf Man, and go on family pack runs, even if he has to put up with all of his little brothers and sisters. They're always howling when he tries to talk! Mom says he has his father's fur. Boy, is he proud of that!

FRANKY STEIN has always been bigger than the other monsters. But it's not just his body that's big. It's his brain and his heart as well. He has plenty of hugs and smiles to go around. His dad, Frankenstein, is the scout-master, and one of Franky's favorite things is his well-worn Junior Monster Scout handbook. One day Franky is going to be a scoutmaster, like his dad. But for now . . . he wants a puppy. Dad says he'll make Franky one soon. Mom says Franky has to keep his workshop clean for a week first.

GLOOMY
WOODS

LAKE

VILLAGE

BARON VON
GRUMP'S HOUSE

CHAPTER
1

"COME ON, FRANKY!" SAID VAMPYRA. "WE'RE missing all the fun!"

"It sounds like a howling good time!" said Wolfy.

"One more bolt to tighten," said Franky. "There! Now my windup monster is all ready for the village's first ever Monster Mash competition!"

The villagers had been so thankful for the Junior Monster Scouts helping them before, that the mayor insisted the Junior Monster Scouts join them for the village's birthday celebration. To show the Junior Monster Scouts that the villagers were no longer afraid of the monsters (it had all been a big misunderstanding), the mayor declared a special contest: a Monster Mash competition. Whoever created the coolest, the craziest, the most wonderful windup monster would win the first place ribbon and a hand-carved cuckoo clock, made by none other than the mayor himself!

Franky set his wrench down and stepped back. His windup mechanical monster hopped up and down, clapping its claws and waving its tentacles.

"That looks great, Franky!" said Wolfy.

"First place ribbon, here I come," said Franky. "That cuckoo clock will look great in my room!"

"Ribbon, schmibbon," said Vampyra. "Party, here I come!"

"I can smell the popcorn from all the way up here!" said Wolfy.

"Smell it all you want," said Franky. "I plan on *tasting* it! Oh, sweet butter, delicious salt . . ."

He closed his eyes and spun in a circle.

"Not if I get there first and eat it all!" teased Vampyra. She flipped her cape around herself and turned into a bat.

Vampyra, Wolfy, and Franky flew, ran, and charged down the road away from Dracula's Castle, hooting, hollering, and howling. They were going to a party tonight, and they were very excited.

Parties are very fun. And birthday parties are even *more* fun. Only, this birthday party was not for just one person. . . . It was for the entire village! The village was one hundred fifty years old today, and they were having a great big birthday party. One hundred fifty is a lot of years, and so there was a lot of celebrating.

Do you know who was *not* celebrating? Do you know who did not like the *pop*, *pop*, *POP* of the popcorn machine? Or the bright lights strung from the tents and buildings? Or the marching band? Or the merry-go-round? Or the sugary scent of fresh birthday cake?

That's right . . . Baron Von Grump. He did not like any of those things.

"Caw! Caw!"

And neither did Edgar, his pet crow.

Baron Von Grump folded his arms. He scrunched his big, black, bushy eyebrows. He glared out his window from the top of the rickety Old Windmill.

"Merry-go-round," he muttered. "There's nothing *merry* about it!"

He picked up his violin and set the bow to the strings, but when he tried to play, the popcorn POPPED!

He tried again. *Pop-pop-POP!* Then the music of the merry-go-round spun round and round, right in through his window.

He marched to the other side of the room,

took a deep breath, set the bow to the strings, and . . . *Pop-pop-POP!* Merry-go-round music. *BOOM-BOOM-BOOM* and trumpets trumpeting, horns blaring as the marching band marched through the village.

"Noise, noise, noise, NOISE!" he bellowed.

A long, high-pitched whistling sounded outside his window, and before he could

close the shutters, a single firecracker landed inside his room.

"This is the last—"

POP! BANG! WHIZ!

"Caw!" said Edgar, flapping straight out the window.

"Straw," grumbled Baron Von Grump, collapsing into his chair.

CHAPTER

2

VAMPYRA, WOLFY, AND FRANKY HAD not made it very far when a loud *BOOM* shook the treetops.

"Was that thunder?" asked Wolfy.

A flash of light lit up the night sky.

"Was that lightning?" asked Vampyra.

A sharp crack and crackle sent jagged sparks across the sky.

"Are those fireworks?" said Franky.

BOOM! FLASH! CRACK! CRACKLE!

"I don't think that's thunder," said Franky.

"Or lightning," Wolfy said.

"Or fireworks," said Vampyra.

Franky, Wolfy, and Vampyra were right. It was *not* thunder, or lightning, or fireworks. And it was *not* coming from the cloudy sky. It was coming from the tallest tower of Castle Dracula, where Franky's grandfather Doctor Frankenstein lived.

A bright green flash of light burst out of the top window of the tower.

"Help!" someone yelled.

"That sounded like my cousin Igor Junior!" said Franky.

"It sounds like he needs our help," said Wolfy.

"If someone is in trouble, better get there on the double!" Vampyra said.

Franky, Wolfy, and Vampyra put their

hands together and said, "Junior Monster
Scouts to the rescue! Let's go!"

They turned right back around and raced
up the road, back to Castle Dracula and
away from the party.

• • •

But not everyone heard the cry for help. Not everyone thought something dangerous might be happening. In fact, the villagers thought the bright lights and loud booms and flashes and crackling crackles were a wonderful, spectacular fireworks show.

They oohed. They aahed. They clapped their hands and whistled.

"What a splendid birthday gift for our village!" said the mayor. "Strike up the band! Sound the flügelhorns!" He cleared his throat and fluffed out his magnificent mustache. "Friends, neighbors, villagers one and all, won't you join me in song?"

Hat in hand, the mayor began.

"*Happy birthday to us, happy birthday to us . . .*"

The whole village joined in. You can join in too, but not yet. We'll come back to the birthday song in a moment. Right now, Igor Junior needs some help.

CHAPTER
3

THE JUNIOR MONSTER SCOUTS RAN UP
and up and up and up and up and up the
stairs. There were a lot of stairs. There were
so many stairs that they had to stop half-
way to catch their breath.

"How many stairs *are* there!?" said Wolfy.
"How tall *is* this tower?"

See? It was a very tall tower with a *lot* of
stairs.

"I'm dizzy," said Franky.

And they were spiral stairs. That means
that they went in a circle, up and up and up
and . . . you get the idea.

When they got to the top of the stairs, they found the door to Doctor Frankenstein's laboratory closed. There was a sign on the door. It read:

AWAY ON MAD SCIENTIST BUSINESS.
PLEASE RETURN TOMORROW.

"Nobody is home," said Vampyra.

Wolfy scratched his head. "But we heard—"

"HELP!"

"That is Igor Junior!" said Franky. "And he's inside!"

Franky gripped the doorknob and pulled. The door did not budge. He grabbed it with both hands and pulled harder. It still did not budge. Wolfy wrapped his arms around

Franky, and they both pulled. It budged a teeny bit. Vampyra wrapped her arms around Wolfy, and all three of them pulled. It budged a teeny bit more.

"Igor Junior!" called Franky.

"Franky?" said Igor Junior from the other side of the door.

"Push the door!" Franky said.

He did. He pushed. They pulled. And then . . . the door popped right open, spilling them all into one tangled pile of monsters.

"We heard your cry for help!" said Vampyra.

"And we rushed here to help you!" said Franky.

"Up a lot of steps," Wolfy grumbled.

Igor Junior wrung his hands. "Thank you, Junior Monster Scouts, but I'm in so much trouble! I don't know if you can help. I don't know what to do!"

"What's wrong?" said Franky.

"Yeah," said Vampyra. "What's the problem?"

Igor Junior pointed back into the laboratory. "Look," he said.

Doctor Frankenstein's laboratory was an absolute disaster. Imagine what your room would look like if you pulled out every toy you had and spread them all over the floor. Then you threw your clothes around your room. Then you pulled every sheet, pillow, blanket, and stuffed animal off your bed. Then you tossed everything up in the air and let it lie where it fell. That would be a disaster. But it would still not be as bad as what the laboratory looked like.

Tables were turned over. Beakers and vials and jars lay on the floor. Gears ground and groaned. Strange coils hissed and spit sparks. Smoke drifted through the room, and green flashes of light pulsed. A jagged bolt of lightning struck the opening in the ceiling, and crackling arcs of electricity raced down the chains dangling from above.

It was a disaster. A *dangerous* disaster.

"What happened?" said Franky.

Igor Junior buried his face in his hands and moaned.

"Pop and Grandpa told me," Igor Junior said. "They told me and told me and told me."

"What did they tell you?" Vampyra said.

"They said, 'Igor Junior, don't touch that lever.'"

"Let me guess . . . ," said Wolfy.

"Yep," said Igor Junior. "I touched that lever."

CHAPTER

4

BARON VON GRUMP STUFFED COTTON IN his ears. He put on earmuffs. He wrapped a scarf around the earmuffs, but still he could not stop all of that noise, noise, noise, NOISE from getting through.

"Stop oohing," he said. "Stop aahing. Stop blaring those flügelhorns and pounding your drums. And above all . . . STOP. SINGING!"

"Caw, caw!" said Edgar.

"What did you say?" asked Baron Von Grump. He unwound the scarf. He took off the earmuffs. He unplugged the cotton.

"Caw, caw!" repeated Edgar.

First Baron Von Grump's big, black, bushy

right eyebrow raised. Then his left. Then, ever so slowly, his lips wriggled into a sly and sinister grin. It was the kind of grin someone gets when they are up to no good.

"That is an excellent idea, Edgar," he said.

"Caw, caw!"

Baron Von Grump clapped his hands together and chuckled. He was definitely up to no good.

"Come, my feathered friend," he said to Edgar. "Let us end this celebration once and for all."

Baron Von Grump and Edgar went down the rickety stairs of the rickety windmill. They went through the crooked door and down the winding trail to a small shack. There was a sign on the door. It read:

VILLAGE POWER

DO **NOT** ENTER

THIS MEANS YOU!

Do you think that Baron Von Grump listened?

You're right; he did not. He did not listen at all. He did not listen, he did not follow instructions, and he certainly was not about to behave himself. He marched right past the sign, right through the door, and right into the small room.

Inside the room was a giant machine. It was the size of a refrigerator, with lots of dials and buttons and one big lever. One side of the lever read: ON. The other side read: OFF.

The switch was in the ON position.

Baron Von Grump gripped the lever.

"Caw, caw!" said Edgar.

"Yes, Edgar," said Baron Von Grump. "On three!"

"Caw . . . caw . . . caw!"

Baron Von Grump pulled the lever.

• • •

Do you remember what we were singing a couple of chapters ago? We were singing "Happy Birthday" to the village. Me, you, the mayor, the villagers—we were all singing. There were flügelhorns and the rest of the band. Remember? Okay, good. Let's try this again.

"*Happy birthday to us, happy birthday to us, happy birthday, dear village, happy birthday to—*"

Suddenly the lights went out. The popcorn machine stopped popping. The merry-go-round stopped going round. Everything was dark and quiet and suddenly not-so-merry.

The party had ground to a halt, and I think you know why.

I'm pretty sure you know who was behind it. But the villagers? They did not.

They had no idea why there was no power. Who might have pulled a lever they were not supposed to pull? Who wanted an end to their party celebrations?

But we know who it was. We know *exactly* who it was, and his initials are B. V. G.

CHAPTER
5

FRANKY, WOLFY, VAMPYRA, AND IGOR Junior stood at the open doorway to Doctor Frankenstein's laboratory.

Thunder boomed, lightning crackled, and the whole room was a hissing, spitting, sparking, grinding, flashing mess!

"So all we have to do is pull that lever back to where it was in the first place?" said Franky.

"Yes," said Igor Junior.

"That lever all the way on the other side of the room?" said Wolfy.

"Yes," groaned Igor Junior.

"Then why didn't you just do that in the first place?" Vampyra said.

"Because I was scared," said Igor Junior.

"I don't blame you," Wolfy mumbled.

Franky pulled out his copy of the Junior Monster Scout handbook and opened to the Scout Laws.

"'It may be scary,'" read Franky, "'but a Junior Monster Scout is brave.'"

"'And that means doing what is right,'" said Vampyra, reading over his shoulder.

"'Even if they are afraid,'" finished Wolfy.

"'*Especially* if they are afraid,'" Franky said. "'That's what being brave is.'"

"You'll help me?" said Igor Junior.

"Of course!" said Vampyra.

Igor Junior puffed out his chest. "Then let's go!" he said.

He reached back and took Franky's hand. Franky took Vampyra's hand. Vampyra took Wolfy's hand, and Wolfy . . . Well, I suppose he would have held your hand if you were there with the Junior Monster Scouts, but you were not. So Wolfy did not hold anyone's hand but Vampyra's.

Slowly but surely they crept through the laboratory. Past the hissing steam pipe. Over the sparking wire. Under the grinding gears. Around the spitting cauldron. And right up to the flashing machine with the big red lever.

"Well, this is the one," said Igor Junior.

"That wasn't so bad," said Wolfy.

Thunder boomed overhead, and an arc

of lightning lit up the sky. All four of them jumped. It was loud, and it was scary. But the Junior Monster Scouts and Igor Junior were being brave. Remember? That means doing something even when you are afraid. They were certainly afraid, but they were going to help Igor Junior, and this time Igor Junior wasn't going to *pull* that lever. . . . He was going to *push* it, right back to where it belonged.

"Go ahead," Vampyra said.

"You can do it," said Wolfy.

Igor Junior wiggled his fingers. He squared his shoulders. He took a deep breath. He reached out for the lever—

"Wait!" said Franky. He held up the Junior Monster Scout handbook and said . . .

CHAPTER

6

WE'LL GET BACK TO WHAT FRANKY said. But for now we are going to go to the village, where everything was dark and confusing and no longer fun.

"What's going on?" asked a villager.

"Who turned out the lights?" another villager asked.

"Why did the popcorn stop popping?" asked a third. "How will we have our Monster Mash competition?"

"Oh, man," groaned a fourth villager. "I really wanted that cuckoo clock."

"Everyone stay calm," said the mayor. "I am sure there is a perfectly good explanation for this."

And there *was* an explanation, but the only person it was good for was Baron Von Grump.

Baron Von Grump trudged back to his crooked windmill with an equally crooked grin on his face.

"Caw, caw!" said Edgar.

"Yes," he said, "of course it is dark. We turned off the power. No power, no lights. No lights, no partying."

"Caw, caw?" asked Edgar.

"I'll simply light a candle," said Baron Von Grump. "A nice, soft, soothing candle by which to play my violin. And this time, nothing will get in my way!"

Okay, hold on. You and I know that is probably not true. You and I know that someone is probably going to get in his

way . . . *three* someones . . . and you know who they are: the Junior Monster Scouts!

Which reminds me . . . weren't we waiting to hear what Franky was about to say? We were, weren't we?

Franky quoted the Junior Monster Scout handbook. . . .

CHAPTER
7

"'A SCOUT IS CAREFUL,'" HE SAID. "'They think about what they are going to do *before* they do it.'"

"Do you think it is dangerous?" said Igor Junior.

"It could be," said Vampyra.

"It sure looks dangerous," Wolfy said. "Look at all of those sparks!"

"If it looks dangerous, it probably is dangerous," said Franky.

"But if we don't turn it off, the whole lab will be ruined!" cried Igor Junior. "That lever controls all of the extra electricity for Doctor Frankenstein's experiments!"

"Maybe we don't need to touch the lever," Franky said. "Maybe we can use something else."

"Something with a long reach," said Wolfy.

"And light enough for Igor Junior to hold," said Vampyra.

"Like this broom!" said Igor Junior. He held up a long push broom. "It's light and has a long reach and just might work!"

More lightning flashed. More thunder boomed. More things sparked and hissed and groaned and creaked and popped and flashed.

"You can do it, Igor Junior," said Vampyra.

Igor Junior reached out with the broom. He pressed it against the lever, and then he pushed.

But nothing happened.

He pushed harder.

But still nothing happened.

He pushed as hard as he could, and *still* the lever did not budge.

"It's stuck," he said. "We'll never budge it."

"Maybe we can help," said Franky.

"Never say 'never' when friends work together!" said Wolfy.

Franky, Vampyra, and Wolfy all grabbed the broom with Igor Junior.

"On three!" said Vampyra. "One . . ."

"Two . . . ," said Wolfy.

"Three!" said Franky.

Igor Junior and the Junior Monster Scouts pushed as hard as they could, and finally the lever moved. It clicked right back to where it was before Igor Junior pulled it.

The sparking, groaning, hissing, creaking, and popping all STOPPED. The lightning stopped flashing. The thunder stopped

booming. Doctor Frankenstein's laboratory was back to normal.

Almost. There was still a lot of mess to clean up.

"We did it!" said Vampyra.

"Thank you, Junior Monster Scouts," said Igor Junior. "But look at this mess! I'm going to be in BIG trouble."

"You're not the only one in trouble right now," said Wolfy. He pointed out the window, toward the village. "Look!"

8

BARON VON GRUMP SETTLED BACK INTO his favorite chair. Edgar settled onto his favorite ceiling beam.

It was dark in the windmill. It was dark everywhere, now that the electricity and lights had all gone out. But it was not a spooky dark, not like the Gloomy Woods from the Junior Monster Scouts' last adventure. This dark was like if you were hiding under your favorite blanket and you couldn't really see anything in detail, just dark, fuzzy shapes. There was enough moonlight to make sure you didn't stub your toe or run into a wall. But otherwise . . . it was pretty dark.

"Now this is more like it," said Baron Von Grump. "This is just what I need. A nice, quiet, soothing place to play my music, and no villagers or Junior Monster Scouts are going to get in my way!"

"Caw, caw!" said Edgar.

"Yes," said Baron Von Grump, "meddlesome Junior Monster Scouts always sticking their claws where they don't belong. But not this time!"

Baron Von Grump shook his fist in the air. He was still upset about the Junior Monster Scouts ruining his last plan. If it weren't for the Scouts, he, Baron Von Grump, would have stopped the villagers' big cheese festival and chased them all away once and for all.

Then he took a deep breath, counted to three, and let it out. This made him feel even more relaxed. It is very important to feel relaxed when you are going to play soothing music. It is also important to stretch before you do activities.

Baron Von Grump stretched his arms out in front of him and spread his fingers wide apart. First he made tiny circles with his thumb. He went in one direction, then the other direction. Then he wiggled both of his pointer fingers, then the middles, then the ring fingers, and finally the pinkies. Then he wiggled them all at the same time.

If you didn't know that Baron Von Grump was stretching his muscles, you might have thought he was casting a spell. But he was not. He was just getting ready to play his violin.

Edgar stretched out his wings and made tiny circles with them. He was not going to play the violin. He was going to clap when Baron Von Grump was finished with his masterpiece song, and he wanted to be ready. He did not want to pull a feather while clapping.

Baron Von Grump unfastened the clasps of his old violin case and opened the lid. A soft ribbon of moonlight covered the polished wood and silvery strings.

Baron Von Grump pulled his violin from

its case. He rested it against his neck and under his chin. He lifted the bow to the strings and took a deep breath. This was the moment he had been waiting for. This was his moment to create his masterpiece, a song that would make him famous. A song that everyone would love! A song that would show everyone just how good he was.

He was about to draw the bow across the strings when he stopped.

"It's too dark," he said.

"Caw?" said Edgar.

"Too dark," said Baron Von Grump. "I cannot see the strings."

"Caw, caw!"

"Yes, I know that I'm the one who made

it dark in the first place," said Baron Von Grump. "That was the idea! But it's a little too dark . . . for me."

"Caw!"

"Another candle!" said Baron Von Grump. "That is an excellent idea!"

Baron Von Grump set his violin down and lit another candle. Now there were two. He placed it upon the open window, next to the first candle, and prepared, once again, to play his violin.

The villagers were not about to sit around and do nothing. They marched right to that power shed . . . and stopped.

The mayor leaned forward and peered at the sign on the door.

"What does it say?" asked a villager.

"It says 'Do not enter,'" said the mayor.

"Does that mean *us*?" asked another villager.

The mayor leaned closer and peered at the sign again.

"It says, 'This means you,'" he said.

"Oh dear," said a third villager. "Now what?"

The mayor held his hat in his hand and turned away from the power shed. "I suppose we'll have to cancel the village birthday party *and* the first ever Monster Mash competition."

CHAPTER
9

FRANKY, VAMPYRA, AND IGOR JUNIOR rushed to the window to see what Wolfy was looking at.

"All I see is darkness," said Igor Junior.

"That's just it," said Wolfy. "There's supposed to be a big birthday celebration for the village."

"With popcorn," Franky said. "And the first ever Monster Mash competition that I worked so hard for."

"And a merry-go-round," said Vampyra. "Let's not forget the merry-go-round."

"That sounds fun," said Igor Junior.

"Exactly," said Wolfy. "But it sure doesn't look like anyone is having fun down there."

"What's everyone looking at?" said a very large rat with a very large belly, munching on a wedge of cheese.

None of the Junior Monster Scouts were surprised to see him. He was the leader of all the rats and lived in the basement of Castle Dracula. He was a very nice rat, even if he had bad manners, like chewing cheese with his mouth open.

"The village," Wolfy said. "There's no birthday celebration."

"It's so dark," said Vampyra.

"Oh yeah," said the rat. He waved his cheese in the air. "The power is out."

Igor Junior peered out the window. "Look!

There's a candle in the Old Windmill!"

"The villagers need light!" said Vampyra. "Electricity!"

"Good thing Doctor Frankenstein has his own power," said Wolfy.

Franky scratched his bolts. He did this when he was thinking really hard. He thought of his mechanical monster for the village's first ever Monster Mash competition. He thought of Doctor Frankenstein's laboratory. He thought of what Wolfy had just said. He thought of the lever that Igor Junior was not supposed to touch but had touched anyway.

"Boris," said Franky. (Boris was the name of the large rat with bad manners.) "Can you gather all the rats and bring them here?"

"What?" asked Boris. "Now? We're having a cheese party!"

"You know what goes great with cheese?" asked Franky.

"More cheese?" Boris asked.

"He has a point," said Wolfy.

"Popcorn," said Franky. "Cheese-covered popcorn."

"Say no more," said Boris. He ran off to gather the rest of the rats.

Wolfy's stomach grumbled and growled. "All this talk of popcorn is making me hungry."

Franky wrapped his arms around his friends. "I've got a plan."

CHAPTER
10

BEFORE LONG, BORIS RETURNED WITH
the rest of the rats. There were a lot of rats.

"So, what's the plan?" asked Boris.

"Yes," said Igor Junior, "what is the plan?"

Franky smiled. "You know all that sparking, popping, spitting, hissing, crackling electricity?" he said.

"You mean the electricity that almost destroyed the laboratory?" asked Wolfy.

"Yes," said Franky. "It just needed some-where to go!"

"Like the village!" said Vampyra.

Igor Junior did not look happy.

"I'm not so sure, Franky," he said. "That would mean I would have to pull that lever *again*."

"But this time you would be pulling it to help someone," said Vampyra.

"A whole village!" Wolfy said.

"And let's not forget what that means," said Boris the rat. "Cheesy popcorn!"

All the rats cheered. They were very excited about anything that had to do with cheese.

"Well, maybe . . . ," said Igor Junior.

"And this time," said Franky, "you won't pull it alone. We'll all do it."

"You will?" said Igor Junior.

"We sure will," said Wolfy.

Franky told them all his plan. It was a good plan, and soon the rats were running through the night, pulling extension cords down from the castle. The rats ran down the Crooked Trail. They ran past the graveyard, through the Gloomy Woods, and across the covered bridge. They ran right to the village, and when they got there, they did just as Franky had said. They plugged their extension cords into the festival lights, and the merry-go-round, and the popcorn machine. Especially the popcorn machine. Nobody could see the rats because it was so dark. And the rats could stay out of everyone's way because rats are very good at sniffing and hearing in the dark. And when they were done, they ran back the way they had come, straight to Castle Dracula.

They were tired. That was a lot of running. But they knew that all that running meant delicious cheesy popcorn. You would probably run back and forth for delicious cheesy popcorn too.

Boris gave Franky a thumbs-up. He was too out of breath to speak.

"Ready?" said Franky.

"Ready," said Igor Junior. He put his hand on the lever.

Wolfy put his hand on the lever too. Then Vampyra added her hand. And finally Franky added his.

"On three," said Franky.

"One . . . ," said Wolfy.

"Two . . . ," said Vampyra.

"THREE!" said Igor Junior. "Pull that lever!"

Igor Junior and the Junior Monster Scouts pulled the lever. A bolt of lightning flickered in the sky. It hit the lightning rod at the

very top of Castle Dracula. It surged down the laboratory cables. It raced along all the extension cords Boris and the rats had taken to the village.

And then?

A tremendous cheer came from the village!

CHAPTER

11

DO YOU KNOW WHY THE VILLAGERS were cheering? I'm sure you do.

Suddenly the lights were on and the village was all lit up. The merry-go-round was going round and round and up and down. The popcorn machine was pop-pop-popping away. The birthday celebration was right back on! The Monster Mash competition was back on schedule!

"Hip, hip, hooray!" cheered the mayor.

"Hip, hip, hooray!" cheered the villagers.

Go ahead—you try it. Give a big cheer. It feels good, right? Well, now you know how the villagers felt. They were very happy to have their birthday celebration back, even if they didn't know how it had happened.

However, not everyone was happy. . . .

Baron Von Grump had been sitting in his chair. He watched the soft glow of the single candle. He held his violin against his neck and shoulder. He took a deep breath, placed the bow against the strings, and—

WHOOM! The lights of the village shone as bright as day, right in his eyes.

The violin made a horrible screech as

Baron Von Grump fumbled the bow across the strings.

SPLOING! Three of his violin strings broke.

"Caw! Caw!" screeched Edgar.

POP-POP-POP-POP went the popcorn machine.

Baron Von Grump tumbled back out of his chair and landed on the floor with a *THUD.*

"Yeow!" he roared.

"Caw! Caw!" hollered Edgar.

Baron Von Grump jumped to his feet, scrunching his thick, black, angry eyebrows together and waving his hands in the air. "Edgar, what do you mean it's the Junior Monster Scouts?"

"Caw, caw!"

"The power is coming from Castle Dracula?"

"Caw, caw!"

Baron Von Grump pulled at his hair. "Why, you Junior Monster Scouts! Wait until I get my hands on—"

Baron Von Grump tripped over his violin and fell face-first onto the floor with an even louder THUD.

"—youuuu," he moaned.

12

"WE DID IT!" SAID IGOR JUNIOR.

"You certainly did!" boomed a very loud, very stern voice. "Look at this place!"

"Dad?" said Igor Junior.

Sure enough, Igor Junior's dad, Igor Senior, stood in the laboratory doorway. And just like Baron Von Grump, he did *not* look happy. He was also not alone. Doctor Frankenstein was with him. So were Dracula, Frankenstein, and Wolf

Man. They also did not look happy. No one was looking happy.

It was a very uncomfortable moment.

"Look at my laboratory!" said Doctor Frankenstein.

"What did I say, Igor Junior?" asked Igor Senior. "I said one thing. I said, 'Igor Junior—'"

"'Do *not* pull that lever,'" mumbled Igor Junior.

"And what did you do?" Igor Senior asked.

"I pulled the lever," said Igor Junior.

"And one more question," said Dracula. "What's with all the rats? I thought they lived in the basement."

"We were promised cheesy popcorn," said Boris.

"Yeah," said the rest of the rats.

Now all the adults did not look as angry.
They looked confused. They had no idea
what cheesy popcorn had to do with
anything, let alone the terrible mess in the

laboratory. And they certainly had no idea why the rats would have been promised cheesy popcorn.

"That's the thing," said Vampyra. "Igor Junior did not pull the lever by himself."

"He didn't?" Igor Senior asked.

"Well, maybe the first time," said Franky. "But then we all pulled the lever."

"You did?" asked Frankenstein.

"Why would you do that?" Wolf Man asked. "Why would you pull the lever when you were told not to?"

"To save the village," said Wolfy. "They needed electricity for their birthday celebration."

"Don't forget the cheesy popcorn!" said Boris.

"And for their popcorn machines," said Igor Junior.

"And lights so they can judge the windup monsters for the first ever Monster Mash competition," Franky said.

"And for their merry-go-round," said Wolfy.

"We were just trying to help," said Vampyra.

All the adults looked at them for a moment. Nobody said anything. They scrunched their eyebrows. They shuffled their feet. They looked at one another.

"Give us a moment, children," said Dracula.

He and the other parents put their heads together in a huddle. They lowered their voices and talked about adult things in very low, adult tones. Sometimes they pointed. Sometimes they shrugged.

"Thanks for standing by me," said Igor Junior to the Junior Monster Scouts.

Franky clapped him on the shoulder. "That's what friends do."

Finally the adults turned back around.

Dracula cleared his throat. "Okay, kids," he said. "Because you were honest and did what you were *not* supposed to do for a good and helpful reason, you are not grounded. You may go to the village birthday celebration *after* you have helped Igor Junior clean up this mess of a laboratory."

"Every bolt, beaker, and bucket of parts," said Doctor Frankenstein.

"And you, Igor Junior," said Igor Senior. "Because you pulled the lever the first time, when you were specifically told *not* to, you are grounded . . ."

Igor Junior's lip trembled. He just nodded and stared at the floor.

"After you enjoy the village birthday celebration and a bucket of cheesy popcorn," finished Igor Senior.

Igor Junior looked up with a surprised smile on his face. "Really?" he said.

"A big birthday bash like this does not happen every day, and you did help make it possible," said Igor Senior. "But starting tomorrow, you'll be doing double chores for a week!"

Igor Junior's lip was no longer trembling.

"Thanks, Pop. And I'm sorry. I'll make sure to listen from now on."

"Well, what are you waiting for?" said Wolf Man. "The quicker you clean, the quicker you get to that party."

"And the cheesy popcorn," said Boris.

Franky, Wolfy, Vampyra, and Igor Junior all put their hands together.

"'Teamwork' on three," Franky said.

"One . . . two . . . three . . . TEAMWORK!" they all shouted.

Igor Junior and the Junior Monster Scouts sprang into action to clean up Doctor Frankenstein's laboratory. Even Boris and the rats helped.

13

IT DID NOT TAKE LONG FOR IGOR JUNIOR and the Junior Monster Scouts to clean up the laboratory. Things go much quicker when everyone lends a hand. Soon the laboratory was just as Doctor Frankenstein and Igor Senior had left it.

"Okay," said Wolf Man, "it looks like you monsters earned your trip to the birthday celebration."

"And the first ever Monster Mash

competition," said Frankenstein. He winked at Franky.

"And that cheesy popcorn," said Igor Senior.

Boris and the rats cheered.

"But be back before sunrise!" said Dracula. He looked at Vampyra. "You know what the sun does to your complexion."

The Junior Monster Scouts, Igor Junior, and the swarm of rats did not waste any time leaving the castle and heading straight for the village.

Peter the piper, their friend from the village, was the first to see them.

"Hello, Junior Monster Scouts!" he said. "I was hoping you would come to the party. I made a very cool monster for the competition!"

"Hi, Peter!" said Vampyra. "This is our friend Igor Junior. And you know the rats. . . ."

Peter did indeed know the rats. He had helped the Junior Monster Scouts lead them out of the village during their last adventure.

"We're only here for some popcorn," said Boris. "Then it's back to the castle for us."

"Come on," said Peter to the rats. "A big bucket of cheesy popcorn, coming right up. Nice to meet you, Igor Junior. You should check out the merry-go-round. It is a lot of fun!"

Igor Junior and the Junior Monster Scouts took his advice. They went round and round and round and up and down and up and down.

"I think I'm getting dizzy," said Wolfy.

"Welcome to the party, Junior Monster Scouts!" said the mayor. "Do we have you to thank for turning on the lights? We almost had to cancel our party . . . *and* the very special, first ever Monster Mash competition!"

"You are very welcome," Vampyra said. "It was Franky's idea."

"Only because Igor Junior pulled the lever and created all that electricity," said Franky.

"Out-of-control electricity," muttered Igor Junior.

"Is that what that was?" asked the mayor. "We thought it was fireworks."

The mayor and the Junior Monster Scouts laughed.

"Let's not forget the rats," Wolfy said. "They helped too!"

"Of course!" said the mayor. "How about joining us in one big round of 'Happy Birthday'?"

The villagers gathered around. The band

marched in with their drums and horns and clanging cymbals. The mayor raised his bullhorn to his lips, and everyone—including the Junior Monster Scouts, Igor Junior, and Boris and the rats—sang.

"*Happy birthday to us, happy birthday to us,*

happy birthday to our village . . . Happy birth-
day to us!"

It was a wonderful, loud, cheer-filled song. It made everyone happy. Well, almost everyone. There was one person who was *not* happy. You know who he is, and we'll come back to him in a moment. But for now, let's sit back and enjoy the big smiles and good cheer of the villagers, the Junior Monster Scouts, and the cheesy popcorn–stuffed rats.

I'll bet you want some cheesy popcorn now, don't you?

Me too. All this talk of cheese and popcorn has me hungry.

Where was I? Oh, yes . . . the birthday celebration. Igor Junior and the Junior Monster

Scouts played games, sang songs, and rode the merry-go-round at least a dozen times. At the end of the party, everyone gathered for the big Monster Mash competition. There were many cool, crazy, wonderful windup monsters. The mayor had a very difficult time choosing. But in the end, the coolest, craziest, most wonderful windup monster belonged to . . . Franky Stein! The mayor hung the first place ribbon around his neck and awarded him his very own, hand-carved cuckoo clock. Peter the piper came in second.

The Junior Monster Scouts had a grand time, and before long it was time to go home. After all, they had promised to be home before sunrise, and a Junior Monster

Scout *always* keeps a promise.

They shook hands, waved good-bye, and promised to visit again soon. They even got balloons before they left. Balloons make everything better, don't you think? And when they got back to the castle, the Junior Monster Scouts promised to visit Igor Junior *after* he was done being grounded.

"Thanks for saving the day, Junior Monster Scouts," said Igor Junior.

"Sure thing. But remember . . . ," said Vampyra.

"What's that?" Igor Junior said.

"Don't pull that lever!" said Vampyra, Franky, and Wolfy at the same time.

Igor Junior and the Junior Monster Scouts all laughed.

CHAPTER
14

"OKAY, JUNIOR MONSTER SCOUTS," SAID Frankenstein. "Time for tonight's scout meeting. We have a little time before the sun is up."

Franky, Wolfy, and Vampyra gathered around the table in the castle dungeon. It was a big table in the middle of a very big dungeon. Dracula and the Wolf Man sat down too.

"I know you were only helping," said

Frankenstein, "but that was a very dangerous laboratory. You could have been hurt!"

"We were very careful," said Vampyra.

"Yeah, we used a broom to touch the
lever instead of our hands," said Wolfy.

"That was good thinking," said Wolf Man.
"Which is why we think you three earned
your Safety Merit Badges."

"For being smart in how you handled a
dangerous situation," said Dracula.

Franky, Wolfy, and Vampyra smiled.

"You also earned your Loyalty Merit
Badge," said Dracula.

"For sticking by Igor Junior and not letting
him take all the blame," Frankenstein said.

"And helping him clean up his mess,"
said Wolf Man.

Franky, Vampyra, and Wolfy all high-fived.

"Okay, scouts," said Wolf Man. "Line up."

Franky, Vampyra, and Wolfy lined up, proudly wearing their Junior Monster Scout sashes. Wolf Man stopped before each of them and pinned on their Safety Merit

Badges. Dracula stopped before each of them and pinned on their Loyalty Merit Badges.

Then Frankenstein cleared his throat. "Ahem," he said. "We have one more badge to present."

"You do?" said Franky.

"I heard that the mayor gave you a first-place ribbon," said Frankenstein.

"And a very fine, hand-carved cuckoo clock," said Dracula.

"Franky won those in the first ever Monster Mash competition!" said Wolfy.

"He made the coolest, craziest, most wonderful windup monster!" Vampyra said.

Frankenstein arched one eyebrow and winked at Franky. "Why don't we wind it up and see how it does?"

Franky gave the winding key one, two, three, four, five big turns and let go. His mechanical monster hopped up and down and back and forth, clapping its claws and waving its tentacles while the music box inside played a haunted tune.

Franky, Wolfy, and Vampyra danced along with it.

"Great job, Franky," said Dracula. "You earned your Gadget Merit Badge for your creation."

Frankenstein pinned the badge on Franky's sash and patted his shoulder. "Good job, Franky. Good job, all three of you!"

"You know what time it is!" said Wolf Man. He leaped up on the table and howled.

"Time to say the Scout oath!" said Dracula. "And get to bed before the sun rises."

Franky, Vampyra, and Wolfy all held hands and said, "I promise to be nice, not scary. To help, not harm. To always try to do my best. I am a monster, but I am not mean. I am a Junior Monster *Scout!*"

And so this particular tale comes to an end.

Almost . . .

CHAPTER
15

BARON VON GRUMP TRUDGED BACK TO the small shack at the edge of the village, the one with the sign on the door that read:

VILLAGE POWER
DO NOT ENTER
THIS MEANS YOU!

"Bah," he said. "I'll bet it was those meddling monsters and their junior scout goodness that ruined my plan."

He opened the door and went in, even though the sign said NOT to enter . . . again.

"Caw, caw!" Edgar said.

"I know what it says!" growled Baron Von Grump. He marched over to the big tall machine with dials and buttons and one big lever.

"Everyone has electricity now but me!" he said. "Me! Baron Von Grump! If those annoying villagers have electricity, then I want electricity."

He traced his crooked finger along the row of buttons until he found the one labeled:

WINDMILL

He pushed the button. "One last step," he said, grasping the lever.

There was a sign hanging on the lever. The sign read: DO **NOT** PULL THIS LEVER!

"Caw, caw!" said Edgar. He flew in circles around Baron Von Grump.

"I am aware of what it says," sneered Baron Von Grump. "Nobody tells Baron Von Grump what to do!"

"Caw!" Edgar said. He flew in circles around the little shack.

"Coward!" yelled Baron Von Grump.

He wrapped his other hand around the lever and—

You know . . . this sounds oddly familiar, doesn't it? What was Igor Junior told? Do you remember? Perhaps we should give Baron Von Grump one final warning. Ready? Okay, one . . . two . . . three:

Baron Von Grump, do NOT pull that lever!

Of course, he did not listen.

"Edgar?" he groaned. "Could you, perhaps . . . *spring* me free?"

JUNIOR MONSTER SCOUT
· HANDBOOK ·

The Junior Monster Scout oath:

I promise to be nice, not scary. To help, not harm.

To always try to do my best. I am a monster, but

I am not mean. I am a Junior Monster Scout!

Junior Monster Scout mottos:

By *paw* or *claw*, by *tooth* or *wing*, Junior
Monster Scouts can do anything!
Never say "never" when friends work together!
By *tooth* or *wing*, by *paw* or *claw*, a Junior
Monster Scout does it all!

Junior Monster Scout laws:

Be Kind—A scout treats others the way
they want to be treated.

Be Friendly—A scout is open to everyone, no matter how different they are.

Be Helpful—A scout goes out of their
way to do good deeds for others . . . without expecting a reward.

Be Careful—A scout thinks about what
they say or do *before* they do it.

Be a Good Listener—A scout listens to what others have to say.

Be Brave—A scout does what is right, even if they are afraid, and a scout makes the right decisions . . . even if no one else does.

Be Trustworthy—A scout does what they say they will do, even if it is difficult.

Be Loyal—A scout is a good friend and will always be there for you when you need them.

Junior Monster Scout badges in this book:

Gadget Merit Badge

Loyalty Merit Badge

Safety Merit Badge

· ACKNOWLEDGMENTS ·

Having rambled through pages of acknowl-
edgments in book 1, *The Monster Squad*, I am
going to keep this much shorter.

As always, I am so grateful for the love,
support, and encouragement from my
wife, best friend, and adventuring part-
ner, Jessica. She not only champions me
and my work, but also challenges me and
inspires me. Thank you, love! I'm so happy
to be on this writing journey together.

Mad respect and admiration for my
superstar editor, Karen Nagel, and the
entire Aladdin team. I know you love these
books as much as I do, and you've really
made my vision become something even

greater than I anticipated. Thank you!

Thank you, Linda Epstein, for your hard work and dedication to the project. You saw it was more than my initial idea and encouraged me to make something more of it. I really appreciate that.

Many thanks to the amazingly talented Ethan Long for his fun, zany, adorable illustrations. Wow! I just want to hug those Junior Monsters!

I want to thank our children, Zachary, Ainsley, Shane, Logan, Braeden, and Sawyer not only for their excitement and pride in our books, but for all of the sacrifices they've had to make and adjustments they've been through. Thank you.

Thank YOU, the readers . . . because

without you, there'd be no book. Or maybe there'd be a book, but no reader. And what good is a good story without a reader? If a tree falls in the forest, and nobody is around to hear it, does it still make a noise? How much wood could a woodchuck chuck if a woodchuck could chuck wood? Anyway, thanks for reading my book!

Finally, a great big thank you to all of the librarians (media specialists), teachers, and parents who battle digital distractions every day and fight to put books in the hands of young readers. Your commitment to reading, imagination, and creativity is SO important. Thank you!

Oh, and thank you, coffee.

WATCH OUT FOR THE NEXT JUNIOR MONSTER SCOUTS ADVENTURE!

JUNIOR MONSTER SCOUTS

by Joe McGee

It's Raining Bats and Frogs!

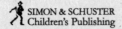 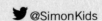